UPSIDE DOWN TALES

THE WOLF'S TALE

DELLA ROWLAND

ILLUSTRATED BY MICHAEL MONTGOMERY

Here is the Wolf's version of this famous story

Turn the book over and read the story from Little Red Riding Hood's point of view

9495·21

A Birch Lane Press Book
Published by Carol Publishing Group
Birch Lane Press is a registered trademark
of Carol Communications, Inc.

Editorial Offices
600 Madison Avenue
New York, NY 10022

Sales & Distribution Offices
120 Enterprise Avenue
Secaucus, NJ 07094

In Canada: Musson Book Company
A division of General Publishing Co. Limited
Don Mills, Ontario

Manufactured in the United States of America

10 9 8 7 6 5 4 3 2 1

Library of Congress Cataloging-in-Publication Data

Rowland, Della
    Little red riding hood and the wolf's tale / by
Della Rowland ; illustrated by Michael Montgomery.
        p.   cm.
        ISBN 1-55972-072-7
        [1. Witches—Fiction.] I. Montgomery, Michael, ill. II. Title.
    PZ7.B5294Han   1991
    [E]—dc20   91-4255
                                                  CIP
                                                  AC

THE WOLF'S TALE

I know you've heard the story of Little Red Riding Hood and the wolf who eats her and her granny. Well, I'm the wolf. William is my name, and I'm going to tell you the real story. First of all, you can see that I didn't fall down dead with a stomach full of rocks. Another thing I want to clear up—I don't eat people. Never have. Chicken is my favorite food—fried, roasted, broiled, barbequed—any kind of chicken. And chicken is what started this whole thing. Here's what happened.

One beautiful summer's day just as I was thinking about some lunch, a little girl in a red cape and hood came skipping through the forest. I noticed she was carrying a picnic basket, and I thought, "Maybe there's something tasty in it—like chicken!" So I ran up the path aways, then turned and walked right up to her.

"Why, hello, little girl," I said as nicely as I could. "My name is William. What's yours?"

"Little Red Riding Hood," she replied.

I thought, "What kind of weird name is *that*?"

"Actually my real name is Rachel," she went on. "But everyone calls me Little Red Riding Hood—or Red. That's because I wear this red cape so much. Isn't it lovely? My granny made it for me."

"Very nice," I smiled. I was trying to pay attention, but it was hard because I could smell roast chicken in her picnic basket. "Tell me, Red," I said, trying not to drool, "are you going on a picnic?"

"No," she said, "I'm taking Granny some roast chicken for lunch."

"Hmmm!" I thought, "not if I can get it first!" Then a brilliant plan came to me!

"You know, Red," I said, "it seems to me that your granny is very good to you. You could show her how much you appreciate her by taking her a bunch of flowers. See those lovely ones over there just beyond the path?"

"Oh, what a good idea," Red exclaimed. "But I don't want to be late for lunch."

"How far away is Granny's house?" I asked.

"It's just on the other side of the woods," Red answered. "It's the one with a red fence and three tall oak trees in front of it."

"So that's where she lives, hmmm?" I replied, rubbing my chin. (Truth was, I knew Granny's house well. She raised the plumpest chickens in the village. I'd stolen quite a few from her.)

"That's not very far," I said. "You could pick a few wildflowers and still get there in time."

"Oh, good!" Red said. Then she set her picnic basket by a tree and skipped off into the forest. As soon as she was out of sight, I pounced on the basket, grabbed the chicken, and raced back to my den. Sitting down, I pulled off a leg—my favorite part—and started to take a bite.

"STOP!" someone screamed—right in my ear!

"AAAHHH!" I yelled, throwing the chicken leg into the air. I whirled around to find Red standing behind me. Then— PLUNK—the chicken leg came down right on my head.

"See what you made me do?" I yelled. "You nearly scared me to death!"

"You stole my chicken!" she shouted.

"Of course, I stole your chicken," I told her. "You shouldn't have left it sitting around."

"I'll bet you're the one who's been stealing chickens from Granny," she said, "and everyone else in the village, too!"

"So what?" I said. "I'm a wolf. Everyone knows that wolves eat chickens. How are we supposed to get them if we don't steal them—raise them ourselves?"

"You know," Red said, "you wolves would be a lot more popular if you stopped eating chickens."

"And just what do you think we would eat?" I demanded.

"Oh, there are lots of good things," she exclaimed. "Here, try a honey cake." And she pulled one out of her basket.

"You expect me to eat that instead of chicken?" I said, looking at the heavy brown biscuit she held out. "Not on your life!"

"Well," Red said sweetly, "I think you'd better, William. Because if you don't stop stealing chickens, I'll tell George where to find you."

I froze. George was a hunter who had been trying to catch me for years. So far I'd always outsmarted him, but with this nosy little girl around, who could say what might happen. After all, she'd followed me to my den without my even knowing.

"No! Wait!" I cried. "All right, I promise I'll stop stealing chickens. Look, I'll even try some of your food."

"Good," she said happily. "I'll bring you breakfast tomorrow."

"Sure," I said. I looked longingly at the chicken as Red packed it up. Then she skipped off. I had no intention of eating her breakfast—tomorrow or any day.

That evening I was nosing around Granny's chickens, as usual. Suddenly I felt a rope catch around one of my hind legs. The next thing I knew, I was swinging high in the air! "George!" I wailed. "You've finally got me!"

Just then I heard, "Hi, William." And up skipped Red. "I knew you wouldn't stop stealing chickens that easily," she said. "But I'll help you break that nasty habit. Here. Have some nice pea soup." Then she opened up her picnic basket and took out a bowl full of thick gloop. And it was green!

"I can't eat green food!" I cried, but she shoved a spoonful in my mouth.

"Pptth!" That's *horrible!*"

"Hush, William,' she said. "You'll love it if you just give it a chance. But you'd better hurry and eat. Mother wants me home

before dark, and I'd hate to leave you hanging here all night. What if George wandered by?"

I hadn't thought about George! Quickly, I slurped up the soup.

"See, William? I told you it was good," Red said, as she let me down. "Tomorrow we'll try something else just as delicious!"

Delicious? No way! My stomach was so upset I could hardly walk. Back at my den I thought, "I'll make an early raid on Granny's chickens tomorrow morning—before Red is even awake!"

I felt a little better when I woke up. But I hadn't gone two feet outside my den when I crashed down into a deep hole that had been covered with brush and grass. "I'm done for!" I groaned. I was sure George had found my den.

But after a moment, Red's smiling face appeared above me. "Good morning, William," she called out cheerfully. "We're going to start the day with some hot oatmeal." She lowered the picnic basket on a rope. "Now eat up."

I opened the basket and took out a bowl. In it was a steaming mound of lumpy gray stuff swimming in melted butter and milk. I'd never seen anything so revolting in my life!

"No!" I said firmly. "I will *never* eat this. *Never!*"

Red peered down the hole at me. "Now, William," she said calmly, "you liked the pea soup once you tried it. You'll like oatmeal, too. But you'd better eat it while it's hot. Cold oatmeal isn't very tasty, as my friend Goldilocks can tell you."

"But I *didn't* like the pea soup!" I howled miserably. I sat in the hole for an hour trying to change her mind, but it was no use. I had to lick the bowl clean before she would throw down a ladder. I limped back into my den and went straight to bed. I was too sick to even *try* to do any chicken stealing.

The next day I moved to another den on the other side of the forest. Then I went to a house far away from Granny's to swipe my lunch. I had grilled my chicken and was just biting into a juicy leg, when Red swooped out of the bushes. Grabbing the chicken leg out of my paw, she stuffed a rice cake with peanut butter into my open mouth. It happened so fast, my teeth were still expecting to bite down on chicken, and they went through the rice cake like nails into a marshmallow. The peanut butter stuck to the roof of my mouth like cement and before I could pull the rice cake off my teeth, Red had run off with *my* chicken.

This was too much! I threw down the rice cake. "I'm a respectable wolf!" I shouted after her. "I eat what respectable wolves eat! Which is NOT peanut butter!"

This went on for weeks. No matter where I moved, Red would find me. Every time I caught a tender little chicken, she'd trap me somehow and make me eat pickled beets or a broccoli omelet. My stomach felt like it had been cut open and filled up with rocks! I was so desperate, I decided to move to another forest.

The road to the next forest went past the village. Wouldn't you know it, I was right in front of Granny's house when I spotted Red behind me. I knew if she saw me she'd think I was trying to steal Granny's chickens. All I could think of was what awful food she might have in her basket and I panicked! I ducked through Granny's front door and ran up the stairs into one of the bedrooms.

"Granny!" I heard Red call out. "Are you home?" Granny wasn't home, so I looked around to see where I could hide. Then I saw one of Granny's nightgowns lying on the rocking chair. "Maybe I can convince Red that I'm Granny and I don't feel well," I thought. "Then she'll go home." Quickly I put on the nightgown and tied on one of Granny's nightcaps.

I jumped into the bed and pulled the covers over my head.

"Pull the latch and let yourself in, child," I squeaked. "I'm too ill to get up."

"Oh, dear," Red cried. I heard her running up the stairs. Then she slowly opened the bedroom door. "Hello, Granny," she said softly. "I've brought you some honey cakes."

"Oh, no," I moaned, "not honey cakes . . . uhh . . . I mean . . . no, no honey cakes yet, dear. Just sit here for a moment."

To my horror, Red climbed right up on the edge of the bed and bent over to give me a kiss. But when she got close to my face, she pulled back and stared at me.

"Why, Granny," she said, "what big arms you have!"

"The . . . ahh . . . better to hug you with, my dear," I replied.

"But, Granny, what big ears you have!" she said.

"The better to hear you with," I said to her.

"But, Granny, what big eyes you have!"

"All the better to see you with, my dear."

"But, Granny, what big teeth you have!"

Before I could stop myself I had said, "All the better to eat CHICKEN with, my dear!"

"Why, you're not Granny!" Red declared. "You're William! What are you doing dressed up in Granny's nightgown?"

I leaped over Red and bounded down the stairs. Just as I reached the door, I ran smack into George and we landed in a heap on the floor.

"Oh, excuse me, Granny," George said, helping me up. "Someone left the front door wide open and I thought I'd better check on you." Then George looked at me.

"Why, Granny," he said, "what big arms you have!"

"Ahh . . . the better to . . . ahh . . . hug you hello, George," I stuttered. "But, Granny," he said, looking me in the eye suspiciously, "what big eyes you have."

"Why, the better to see you . . . ahh . . . without my glasses, George," I said. Then George pulled off my nightcap. "But, William," he bellowed out, "what big EARS you have!"

"The better to hear you with, George," I said. "In fact, you don't have to shout."

This was the most embarrassing moment of my entire life. I had outsmarted George for years. Now he had caught me. And here I was—a respectable wolf— wearing a nightgown! And I was too weak to even try to get away.

"William, you old rascal," George said, chuckling. "I've been tracking you for a long time and now I've got you." And he raised his gun and aimed it right at me.

Well, when I saw the end of George's gun one inch away from my nose, all my strength suddenly came back. I lunged to one side and headed for the door. But I guess George was standing on the nightgown, because when I bolted past him, his feet flew out from under him and down he went and BLAM went the gun, shooting a big hole in Granny's ceiling.

Just then Granny came running in the back door. "Why, look at my ceiling!" she cried. "You should be ashamed of yourself, George Hunter, shooting off your gun in the house."

LITTLE RED RIDING HOOD

AS TOLD BY
DELLA ROWLAND

ILLUSTRATED BY MICHAEL MONTGOMERY

Here is Little Red Riding Hood's version of this famous story
Turn the book over and read the story from the Wolf's point of view

Ariel Books

A Birch Lane Press Book
Published by Carol Publishing Group

A Birch Lane Press Book
Published by Carol Publishing Group
Birch Lane Press is a registered trademark
of Carol Communications, Inc.

Editorial Offices
600 Madison Avenue
New York, NY 10022

Sales & Distribution Offices
120 Enterprise Avenue
Secaucus, NJ 07094

In Canada: Musson Book Company
A division of General Publishing Co. Limited
Don Mills, Ontario

Manufactured in the United States of America

10 9 8 7 6 5 4 3 2 1

Library of Congress Cataloging-in-Publication Data

Rowland, Della
    Little red riding hood and the wolf's tale / by
Della Rowland ; illustrated by Michael Montgomery.
        p.   cm.
        ISBN 1-55972-072-7
        [1. Witches—Fiction.] I. Montgomery, Michael, ill. II. Title.
    PZ7.B5294Han   1991
    [E]—dc20   91-4255
                                                              CIP
                                                              AC

LITTLE
RED
RIDING
HOOD

Once upon a time, there lived a little girl who was so clever and charming that everyone loved her. But her grandmother loved her the most. Her granny made her many lovely things to wear, but the little girl's favorite was a red velvet cloak and hood. She wore the cloak and hood so much that everyone called her Little Red Riding Hood.

Now, this little girl lived with her mother in a cottage near a great forest. And on the other side of the forest lived her grandmother. One day Little Red Riding Hood's mother gave her a basket of honey cakes and oranges to take to Granny.

"Take these cakes and fruit to Granny," her mother said. "She has a cold and they will make her feel better. Fix her a pot of tea when you get there, and don't look through every drawer in her house for candy." Then her mother said sternly, "Now go straight to Granny's, my darling. Don't wander off the path or speak to strangers."

Little Red Riding Hood put on her red velvet hood and she set off through the woods for Granny's house. She hadn't gone far when she met up with a big gray wolf. Little Red Riding Hood had never met a wolf before.

"Good morning, little girl," the wolf crooned. "And where are you off to so early?"

Forgetting all about her mother's warning, Little Red Riding Hood answered, "Why, I'm off to Granny's. She has a cold and I'm taking her some honey cakes and oranges."

"What a good girl," said the wolf. "And tell me, where does your granny live?"

"Not far," replied Little Red Riding Hood. "Just on the other side of the woods. Her house has a red fence and three tall oak trees in front of it."

"Oh, yes," said the wolf. "I know her house well."

Now, the wolf had not eaten for three full days and he couldn't help noticing how plump Little Red Riding Hood was. The rascal thought to himself, "If I am clever, I can have this little girl for dinner—and her granny, too." So he walked a bit with Little Red Riding Hood while he thought up a plan. At last one came to him.

"Just look at the lovely flowers there beyond the path," the wolf said. "I'll bet a bunch of them would perk up your granny like nothing else."

"Oh, what a good idea!" Little Red Riding Hood exclaimed. And she skipped off into the forest.

Licking his lips, the sly gray wolf trotted on down the path. In no time he was knocking on Granny's door—*TOC TOC*.

"Who is there?" the old woman called.

"Little Red Riding Hood," squeaked the wolf in the highest voice he could make.

"Oh, child," Granny said, "just lift the latch and come in so I don't have to get out of bed."

So the wolf did just that. He crept up the stairs to Granny's bedroom. Then he threw open the bedroom door and pounced on the old woman and ate her up before she could even say "Wolf!"

Next the wolf put on one of Granny's nightgowns. After he had tied on one of her night caps, he hopped up into her bed and pulled the covers over his face.

Meanwhile, Little Red Riding Hood had wandered far from the path. She had no sooner picked one flower, than she spotted an even lovelier one just a little farther away. At last, she had gathered so many flowers that she could hardly carry them all.

"These should cheer up my granny," she thought as she hurried back to the path. Soon she reached Granny's house and knocked on the door—*TOC TOC*.

"Who's there?" the wolf called out.

"It's me, your Little Red Riding Hood," the girl answered. Then she thought, "Oh my, how hoarse poor Granny sounds. She must be sicker than Mother thought."

"Pull the latch and let yourself in, dear," the wolf coughed. "I'm too ill to get up."

"Oh dear!" Little Red Riding Hood cried, pulling the latch. Without even stopping to close the door, she ran up the stairs to Granny's bedroom and tiptoed over to the bed.

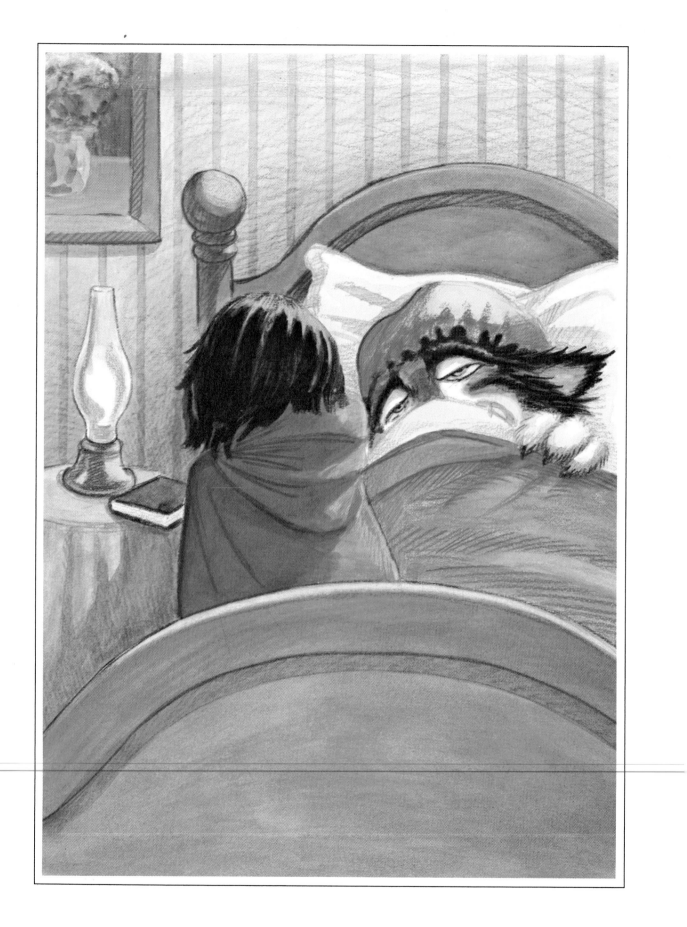

"Hello, Granny," she said. "I've brought you honey cakes and oranges. Would you like some tea?"

"Not yet," the wolf whispered. "Put your basket down, dear girl, and sit on the bed beside me."

So Little Red Riding Hood climbed up on the edge of the bed. But when she leaned over to give her grandmother a kiss, she was astonished at how strange Granny looked. She sat up again quickly.

"Why, Granny," she exclaimed, "what big arms you have!"

"The better to hug you with, my dear," replied the wolf.

"But, Granny, what big ears you have!" the girl said.

"All the better to hear you with," was the reply.

"But, Granny, what big eyes you have!"

"The better to see you with, my dear."

"But, Granny, what big teeth you have!"

"All the better to EAT you with!" snarled the wolf.

And with that he threw off the covers and swallowed Little Red Riding Hood in one gulp!

Now, the wolf should have run away then, and no one would have been the wiser as to what he had done with Little Red Riding Hood and Granny. But his full belly made him drowsy and foolish and he lay back down in the bed. Soon he was fast asleep and snoring loudly.

Just then a huntsman passing by noticed that Granny's door was wide open. "I'd better see if she is all right," he thought. As he walked in the door, he was amazed to hear loud snores coming from the bedroom. "My, how can such an old woman snore so loudly," he thought. But when he opened the bedroom door, he saw that it was not Granny but the wolf lying there.

"Ah ha, you wiley wolf!" he said softly. "I've been tracking you a long time and now I've *got* you!" And he raised his gun to shoot the wolf then and there.

Just as he was about to fire, he realized that Granny was nowhere to be seen. "I'll bet the wolf has eaten her," he thought. Quickly he took his hunting knife and cut open the wolf's stomach. To his surprise, out popped not only Granny but Little Red Riding Hood, too.

Then the huntsman and Little Red Riding Hood filled the wolf's belly with large stones and sewed him back up while he still slept and snored away. When the wolf awoke and saw the huntsman, he tried to run away. But the stones were so heavy that he fell down dead.

Everyone was very happy now. Little Red Riding Hood made tea and the three of them ate the honey cakes and oranges she had brought. By then Granny was feeling much better and it was time for Little Red Riding Hood to return home before it got dark.

Little Red Riding Hood went straight home, without stopping for anything on the way. She vowed to herself, "From now on, I will listen to my mother. I will never speak to strangers or leave the path again when I am by myself." And she never did.

Now, that's the way we've always heard the story of Little Red Riding Hood. But did you know that the wolf tells the story a little differently? Would you like to read what the wolf has to say about the matter? Then turn this book over!